For Isabelle, Joey, Iona, and Callan

Published by
PEACHTREE PUBLISHING COMPANY INC.
1700 Chattahoochee Avenue
Atlanta, Georgia 30318-2112
PeachtreeBooks.com

Text and illustrations © 2021 by Jessica Meserve

First published in the United Kingdom in 2021 by Macmillan Children's Books, an imprint of Pan Macmillan
The Smithson, 6 Briset Street, London EC1M 5NR
Associated companies throughout the world
www.panmacmillan.com

First United States version published in 2022 by Peachtree Publishing Company Inc.

The illustrations were created digitally and using mixed media.

Printed in November 2021 in China

10 9 8 7 6 5 4 3 2 1
First Edition
ISBN 978-1-68263-375-5

Catalog-in-Publication Data is available from the Library of Congress

JESSICA MESERVE

BEYOND THE BURROW

PEACHTREE

ATLANTA

Rabbits love staying close to home.

And home for a rabbit is a burrow
where it is warm and safe and cozy.

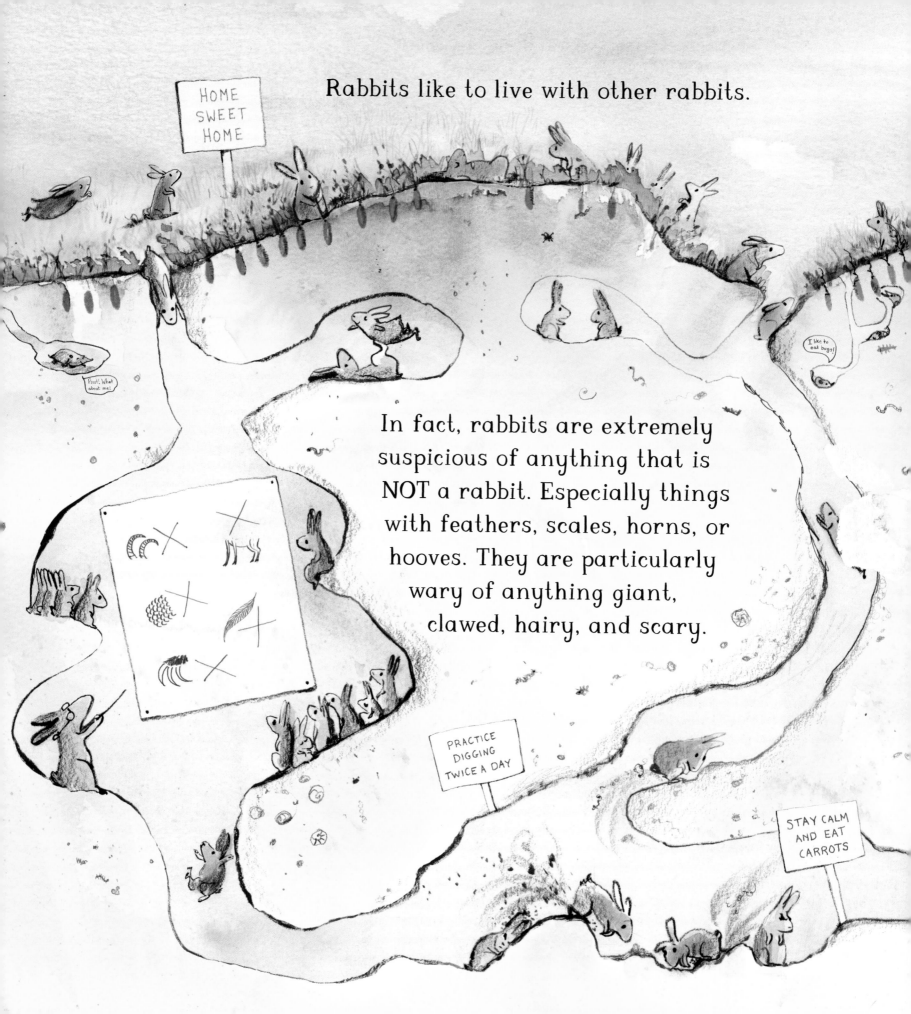

Rabbits like to live with other rabbits.

In fact, rabbits are extremely suspicious of anything that is NOT a rabbit. Especially things with feathers, scales, horns, or hooves. They are particularly wary of anything giant, clawed, hairy, and scary.

Rabbits stick to what they know.
As well as loving to stay home and hopping
around, rabbits also adore carrots.

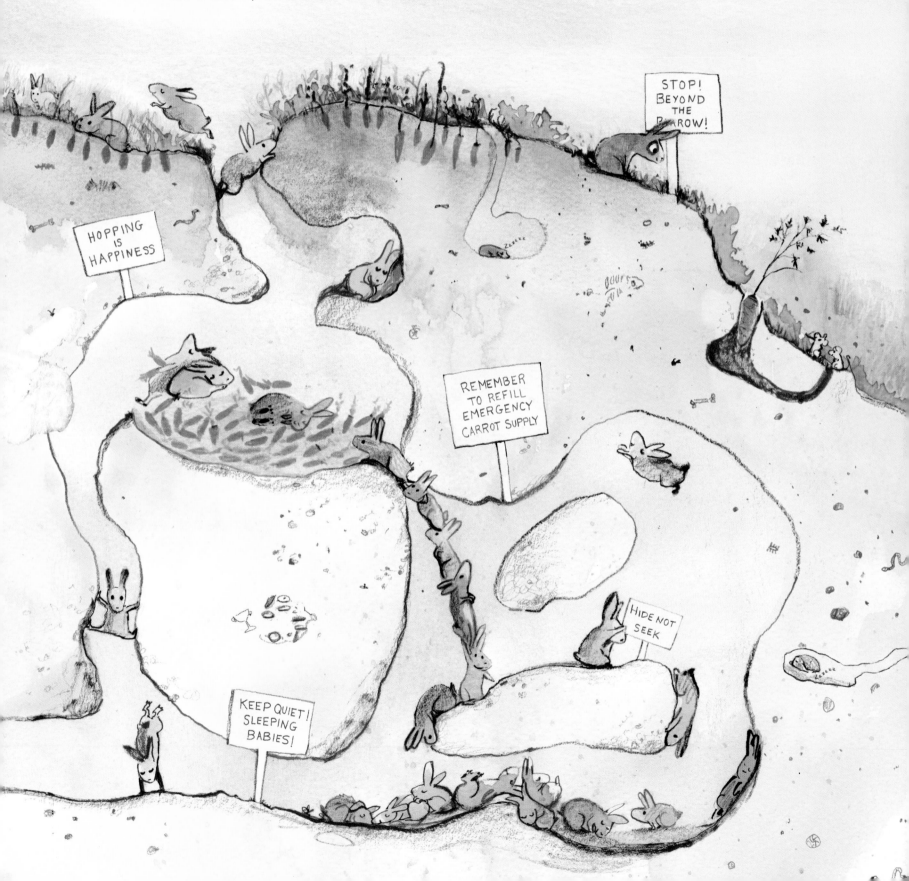

One morning, Rabbit
found the sweetest carrot—
perfect for breakfast!

It was only a whisker
out of reach.

She stretched one little paw,
just beyond the burrow.

Then two...

Then four...

Until...

She tumbled
and rolled
and fell...

WATCH OUT!

UNKNOWN
AHEAD!

LAST
WARNING!

...down the WRONG hole!

Falling is NOT a very
rabbity thing to do.
In fact, it's something
of a disaster.

It isn't warm, it isn't safe, and it *certainly* isn't cozy.

And just when Rabbit thought things couldn't get any worse…

...they did.

Getting wet is
NOT a very
rabbity thing
to do.

Nor is holding
your breath.

Or clinging
to a log.

But this little rabbit didn't have much choice. She clung on tightly until finally she came to a stop, far, *far* beyond the burrow.

At least I haven't met anything that is NOT a rabbit, she thought.

SOMEWHERE NEW!

But then she did.

And this not-rabbit looked giant and clawed and hairy, and *most certainly* scary. But Rabbit didn't wait to find out if it really was.

She did the only rabbity thing she could.

She hopped...

and she dug...

...and she hid.

This was not at all like home! It was cold and damp and frightening!

Rabbit's paws ached and soon her tummy started rumbling.

What if the not-rabbit is hungry too? she thought. *What if it eats ME for breakfast?*

But it didn't.

In fact, it left something behind.

It was NOT a carrot.

Rabbit was very suspicious.

But she was also very, *very* hungry.

She took one nibble…

It was the most delicious thing she had ever tasted!

Then Rabbit had a very new and very bold thought.

Maybe not-rabbits and not-carrots are okay after all!

But how could she find out for sure?

Just then, she heard strange sounds coming from above.

Rabbits are not usually brave and they don't usually climb.

But it *had* been a non-rabbity kind of day.

So up Rabbit went...

...and when she reached the top she said,

"Thank you!"

"You're welcome!" said the not-rabbit.

It was giant, clawed and hairy—but not so very scary.

There were other
not-rabbits in the trees
too. Some with horns
and hooves, some with
beaks and feathers, and
others with fur, teeth,
scales, and tails!

They all gave her the warmest of welcomes. They even offered their favorite snacks! So Rabbit did something kind in return.

She showed them how to hop. Some of them were quite good at it!

Then, feeling much braver,
Rabbit tried hanging...

swinging,

camouflaging,

dancing,

and even flying!

Now this *could* have been a disaster...

...but it wasn't!

*Falling, thought Rabbit,
is fun when you know
there's a soft landing.*

That night, Rabbit couldn't sleep.
She thought about home and how
much she missed the burrow.
It felt so very far away.

Will I ever find it again?
she wondered.

But as the sun rose, she spotted a familiar hill shining in the distance.

And now a much, *much* braver rabbit decided to head for home.

She wasn't sure how
to get there.

The journey was long...

and difficult.
But...

...even the
wrong hole

was less scary

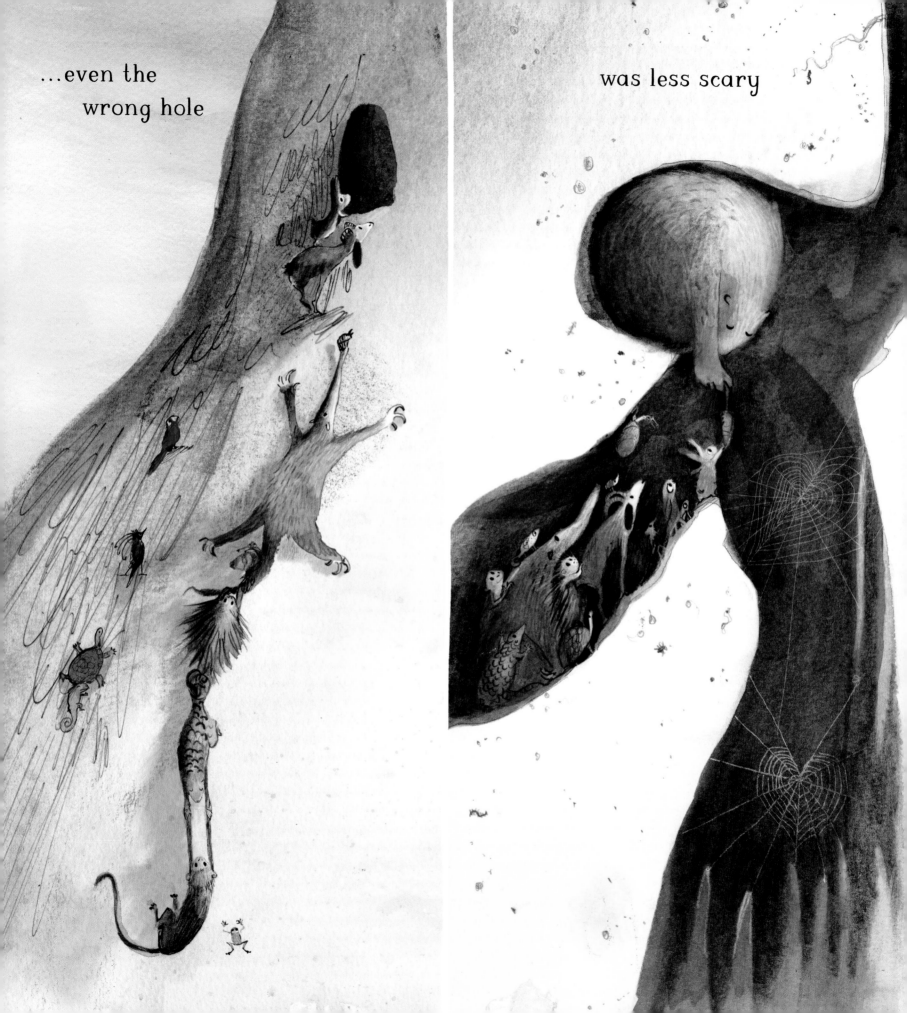

with friends.

As Rabbit led the way, bounding toward
the burrow and the sweet scent of carrots,
she thought things couldn't get any better.

But they did!